Mary Beth Owens

Panda *Whispers*

Dutton Children's Books

Special thanks to Robyn and Bobby for their help.

DUTTON CHILDREN'S BOOKS
A division of Penguin Young Readers Group

Published by the Penguin Group
Penguin Group (USA) Inc., 375 Hudson Street, New York, New York 10014, U.S.A.
Penguin Group (Canada), 90 Eglinton Avenue East, Suite 700, Toronto, Ontario, Canada M4P 2Y3
(a division of Pearson Penguin Canada Inc.)
Penguin Books Ltd, 80 Strand, London WC2R 0RL, England
Penguin Ireland, 25 St Stephen's Green, Dublin 2, Ireland
(a division of Penguin Books Ltd)
Penguin Group (Australia), 250 Camberwell Road, Camberwell, Victoria 3124, Australia
(a division of Pearson Australia Group Pty Ltd)
Penguin Books India Pvt Ltd, 11 Community Centre, Panchsheel Park, New Delhi - 110 017, India
Penguin Group (NZ), Cnr Airborne and Rosedale Roads, Albany, Auckland 1310, New Zealand
(a division of Pearson New Zealand Ltd)
Penguin Books (South Africa) (Pty) Ltd, 24 Sturdee Avenue, Rosebank, Johannesburg 2196, South Africa
Penguin Books Ltd, Registered Offices: 80 Strand, London WC2R 0RL, England

Library of Congress Cataloging-in-Publication Data
Owens, Mary Beth.
Panda whispers / by Mary Beth Owens.—1st ed.
p. cm.
Summary: Just like the many animal parents who wish their babies good dreams
at bedtime, a human father wishes sweet dreams to his child.
ISBN 978-0-525-47171-4 (alk. paper)
Special Markets ISBN 978-0-525-42052-1 Not for Resale
[1. Bedtime—Fiction. 2. Animals—Fiction. 3. Parent and child—Fiction.
4. Dreams—Fiction. 5. Stories in rhyme.]   I. Title.
PZ8.3.O975Pan 2007   [E]—dc22   2006014504

Published in the United States by Dutton Children's Books,
a division of Penguin Young Readers Group
345 Hudson Street, New York, New York 10014
www.penguin.com/youngreaders
Designed by Abby Kuperstock and Justine Zwiebel
Manufactured in China

For my father, who whispered,
"Think happy thoughts."

In the treetops, by the river,
on the mountains, plains, and sea,
creatures settle down to sleep and
dream sweet dreams, like you and me.

On a mountain, mist is settling.
Panda cuddles with her cub.
Pointing to the tallest tree,
she gives his back a gentle rub.

Panda whispers, *"Dream of climbing."*

Resting in the rolling ocean,
sleepy dolphins close their eyes.
High above, a golden moon
is tossed into the starlit sky.

Dolphin whispers, *"Leap up higher!"*

Hidden in the waves of grass,
Cheetah and her kittens lie.
As they sleep and dream of running,
storm clouds race across the sky.

Cheetah whispers, *"Fast as lightning!"*

On a sparkling hill of sea ice,
rocking on his father's toes,
drowsy little Penguin dreams
of sliding everywhere he goes.

Penguin whispers, *"Use your belly."*

From a treetop in the forest
Lemur rocks her babies three.
Watching branches swing and sway,
they dream of leaping tree to tree.

Lemur whispers, *"Hold on tight."*

In the tallest mango tree,
sheltered from the noonday sun,
mother Fruitbat and her pup
sleep and dream of nighttime fun.

Fruitbat whispers, *"Swooping down."*

Underneath a shooting star,
Llamas hum near mountains steep,
dreaming of the things they'll find
waiting at the highest peak.

Llama whispers, *"Top of the world!"*

Reeds are stirring in the river.
Alligator's smiling wide.
Hatchlings resting on their mother
dream of where they're going to hide.

Alligator whispers, *"I can't see you."*

In the shadows near the water,
Swan and cygnets on their nest
dream of nibbling lily roots
after waking from their rest.

White Swan whispers, "Bottoms up,"

Cradled in a bed of seaweed,
Otter pup and mother sleep.
Round about them clouds of bubbles
rise up from the ocean deep.

Otter whispers, *"School of minnows!"*

In a den beside the meadow,
stars above are shining bright.
Mother Fox and kit awaken
to the curious sounds of night.

Red Fox whispers, *"You'll find crickets."*

Snug within a cozy nest,
restless mice are settling down,
dreaming of the tasty seeds
and hidden berries to be found.

Field Mouse whispers, *"You'll help find them."*

In a bedroom, child and father
hear the ocean in the night.
"Dream you'll sail to far-off places,
then sail back by morning's light."

Father whispers,
    "I'll be waiting here. . . .

"Good night."